SEE THAT CD OVER THERE?

When you play it, I hope you'll be inspired to sing and dance along! Here's a game to get things shakin':

Invite some friends over and pop the CD into a CD player. Pick a leader to start and stop the music. When the leader starts the music, everyone dances like crazy in the middle of the room. When the leader stops the music, the dancers quickly sit down on the floor.

The last person to sit moves to the side of the room and dances there when the music starts again, while the rest of the group continues to dance together. Each round will move one more person to the side group, until the very fastest sitter is left all alone in the middle of the room. That super swift sitter gets to be the next leader so the game can start all over again!

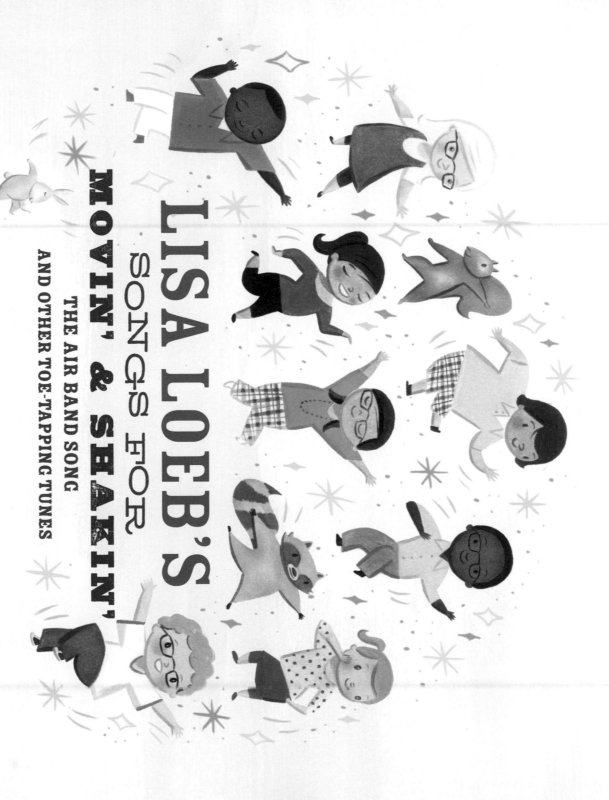

LISA LOEB'S
SONGS FOR
MOVIN' & SHAKIN'

THE AIR BAND SONG
AND OTHER TOE-TAPPING TUNES

ILLUSTRATED BY RYAN O'ROURKE

STERLING CHILDREN'S BOOKS
New York

To my sister, Debbie, who inspires me with her high energy
and her deep understanding that we learn just as much (if not more!)
while we're in motion as we do when sitting still.

To my daughter, Lyla, who loves to sing, jump, and spin.
And to my son, Emet, who is just learning.

STERLING CHILDREN'S BOOKS
New York

An Imprint of Sterling Publishing
387 Park Avenue South
New York, NY 10016

STERLING CHILDREN'S BOOKS and the distinctive Sterling Children's Books logo are trademarks of Sterling Publishing Co., Inc.

Text © 2013 by Lisa Loeb

Illustrations © 2013 by Ryan O'Rourke

Art direction and design by Jennifer Browning

The artwork for this book was prepared using oils and acrylic on illustration board and wood, with some help from Photoshop and Illustrator.

ISBN 978-1-4027-6916-0

Library of Congress Cataloging-in-Publication Data

Loeb, Lisa, 1968-

Lisa Loeb's songs for movin' & shakin' : The air band song and other toe-tapping tunes / illustrated by Ryan O'Rourke.

v. cm.

Includes activities and choreography.

Contents: Turn it down (The air band song) -- Father Abraham -- Miss Mary Mack -- Monster stomp -- Going away --
Everybody wake up -- Hello, today -- Peanut butter and jelly -- Head, shoulders, knees, and toes.

ISBN 978-1-4027-6916-0 (hardcover)

1. Children's songs, English--United States--Texts. [1. Songs.] I. O'Rourke, Ryan, ill. II. Title. III. Title: Songs for movin' & shakin'. IV. Title: Lisa Loeb's
songs for movin' & shakin'.

PZ8.3.L8244Li 201

782.42--dc23

[E]

2012014293

Distributed in Canada by Sterling Publishing
c/o Canadian Manda Group, 165 Dufferin Street
Toronto, Ontario, Canada M6K 3H6

Distributed in the United Kingdom by GMC Distribution Services
Castle Place, 166 High Street, Lewes, East Sussex, England BN7 1XU

Distributed in Australia by Capricorn Link (Australia) Pty. Ltd.
P.O. Box 704, Windsor, NSW 2756, Australia

For information about custom editions, special sales, and premium and corporate purchases,
please contact Sterling Special Sales at 800-805-5489 or specialsales@sterlingpublishing.com.

Manufactured in China

Lot #:
2 4 6 8 10 9 7 5 3 1
01/13

www.sterlingpublishing.com/kids

NOTE FROM Lisa

Although I love to sit down to read a good book,
this book is written to make you get up out of your chair!
Some of the songs are from my Camp Lisa CD, some are
traditional favorites, and others were written with my pals Michelle
and Dan. Every song was chosen with maximum movement
in mind. Teach these songs to your friends, your neighbors,
your pets. . . . Soon you'll have your whole
neighborhood movin' and shakin'!

TURN IT DOWN!
(The AIR BAND SONG)

BASS Guitar

JAZZ FLUTE

GUITAR

Even if you can't play an instrument, you can pretend to play one. You can also use objects in your house to play in your pretend band. That's what my brothers and sister and I used to do before we learned to play real instruments. A tennis racket makes a great guitar!

In this song, each time an instrument is mentioned, play it! Some people call this "air guitar" or "air drums" because you're just playing the imaginary instruments in the air.

DRUMS

Piano

I'm gonna start a band.
I wanna start it now.
I don't have a guitar,
but I'm gonna play it anyhow.
(Guitar break)

No one's gonna tell you you're playin' too loud.
No one's gonna tell you to turn it down.

I'm gonna start a band.
I wanna start it now.
I really need some drums,
and I'm gonna rock 'em out!
(Drum break)

No one's gonna tell you you're playin'
too loud. No one's gonna tell you to
turn it down. Playin' in a band beats
lyin' around, and no one's gonna tell
you to turn it down.

What else do we need to make
our band sound more complete?
Pick up anything around
and play the song along with me,
play the song along with me.
(All instruments jam break)

I'm gonna start a band.
I'm gonna play along:
A jazz flute solo's
gonna sound so wrong!
(Jazz flute break)

I'm gonna start a band.
I'm gonna start it now.
I wanna play the bass,
and I'm gonna lay it down.
(Bass guitar break)

I'm gonna start a band.
I'm makin' up a song:
I'm gonna play piano,
plinky plinky plonk.
(Piano break)

No one's gonna tell you you're playin'
too loud. No one's gonna tell you to
turn it down. Playin' in a band beats
lyin' around, and no one's gonna tell
you to turn it down.

Father Abraham

When you sing this song, get ready to move! Each time a part of your body is mentioned, you have to start moving it, and you can't stop until the song is over. You can add your own movements, too, and make the song longer.

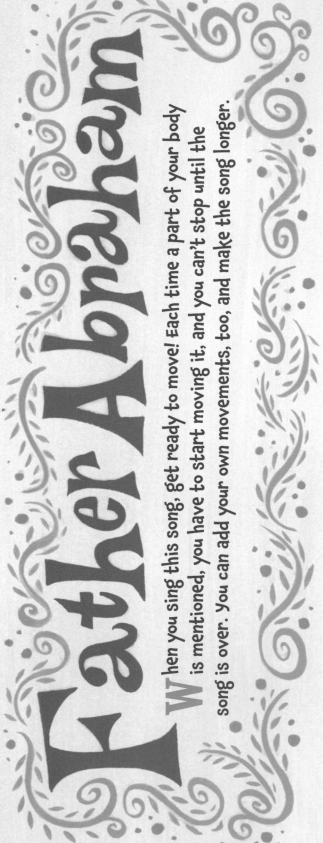

Father Abraham had seven sons, and seven sons had Father Abraham. And they never laughed (**HA HA!**) and they never cried (**BOO HOO!**). All they did was go like this: with the right arm.

Father Abraham had seven sons, and seven sons had Father Abraham. And they didn't laugh (**HA HA!**) and they didn't cry (**BOO HOO!**). All they did was go like this: with the left arm and a right arm.

Father Abraham had seven sons, and seven sons had Father Abraham. And they never laughed (**HA HA!**). They didn't cry (**AWWWW**). All they did was go like this: with the left arm and a right arm and a left leg.

TIP: If you're having trouble telling your left from your right, remember that only your **LEFT** hand can make an "L" shape with your thumb and pointer finger.

Left

Father Abraham had seven sons, and seven sons had Father Abraham. And they never laughed **(HA HA!)** and they never cried **(BOO HOO!)**. All they did was go like this: with the left arm and a right arm and a left leg and a right leg.

Father Abraham had seven sons (seven sons!), and seven sons had Father Abraham. And they didn't laugh **(HA HA!)** and they didn't cry **(BOO HOO!)**. All they did was go like this: with the left arm and a right arm, with a left leg and a right leg, turn around.

Father Abraham had seven sons (seven sons!), and seven sons had Father Abraham. And they never laughed **(HA HA!)**. They didn't cry **(BOO HOO!)**. All they did was go like this.

ADD YOUR OWN MOVES!

{Nod your head}

{Blink your eyes}

{Crawl around}

{Jump up high}

miss mary mack

This is a perfect rhyme for jumping rope or playing a hand-clapping game. You need two people to play, and whoever gets through the rhyme without messing up is the winner. There are only six basic moves, but until you really learn it well, it's a challenge. A fun one! To make it extra tricky, speed up the rhyme each time you repeat it until one of you loses the rhythm.

Miss Mary Mack, Mack, Mack
all dressed in black, black, black
with silver buttons, buttons, buttons
all down her back, back, back.
She asked her mother, mother, mother
for 50 cents, cents, cents
to see the elephants, elephants, elephants
jump over the fence, fence, fence.
They jumped so high, high, high
they reached the sky, sky, sky
and they didn't come back, back, back
till the 4th of July, ly, ly!

MISS

{Cross your arms and touch your shoulders}

MACK

{SLAP your right hand to the other person's right hand, then both CLAP!}

{CLAP}

MA-

{SLAP your thighs}

MACK

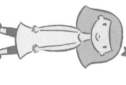

{SLAP your left hand to the other person's left hand, then both CLAP!}

{CLAP}

-RY

{CLAP}

MACK

{Switch back to slapping your right hand to their right hand}

YOU AND YOUR FRIENDS
CAN MAKE UP YOUR OWN
CLAPPING PATTERN.
YOU CAN INCLUDE
THE FLIP-FLOP HAND
SLAP INSTEAD OF
CROSSING ARMS AND
SLAPPING THIGHS.

SLAP

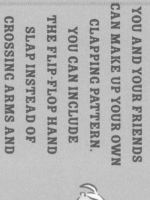

{SLAP palm to palm}

SLAP

{SLAP back of hand to back of hand}

MONSTER STOMP

How to scare away a monster (or anything else that scares you) as taught by the monsters themselves:

1. STOMP THE GROUND.
2. WAVE YOUR ARMS AROUND.
3. LET OUT A GREAT BIG GROWL...

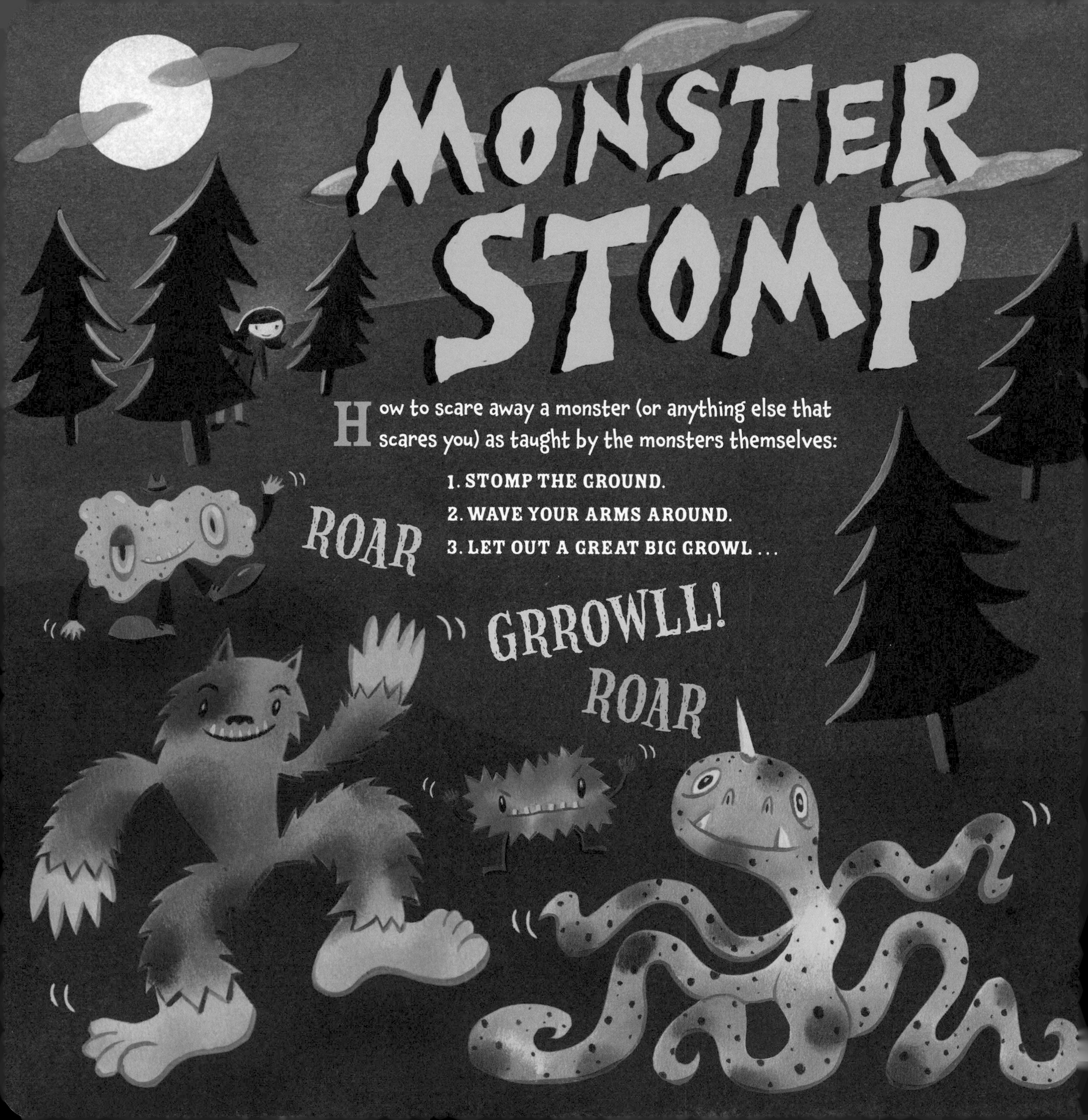

ROAR

GRROWLL!

ROAR

ROAR

Alone in my room on a moonlit night
I heard a scary noise from the woods outside.
I heard a stomp, stomp, stomp, and a giant growl,
saw a shadow move beneath the parting clouds.

First we stomp the ground,
and wave our arms around,
let out a great big growl . . . (ROAR!!!!)
We're doing the monster stomp!

So I went downstairs, creeping quietly,
tip-toed to the woods and hid behind a tree.
There were a bunch of monsters dancing on the forest floor
waving at the moonlight making horrible roars.

So we danced till the night got very late
and the music made the whole forest shake.
They told me, "Kiddo, anytime you feel afraid
you just stomp, stomp, stomp,
and wave and roar,
and chase the monsters away."

First they stomped the ground,
waved their arms around,
let out a great big growl . . . (ROAR!!!)
They were doing the monster stomp!

So now any time I hear a scary noise outside
I don't have to run away and hide.
It doesn't bother me a bit;
I do the dance that the monsters did.

So I left the safety of my hiding tree,
marched straight to the middle of that monster soiree,
and said, "Do ya mind? Can you keep it down?
I'm trying to sleep, and you're really, really loud!"

First I stomp the ground,
and wave my arms around.
let out a great big growl . . . (ROAR!!!!)

Then they all got quiet and they hung their giant heads.
They said, "We're really sorry that we got you out of bed.
But now that you're here, is there any chance
you'd like to learn how monsters dance?"

First I stomp the ground,
I'm doing the monster stomp! (ROAR!!!!)
Chasing the monsters off! (ROAR!!!!)
I'm chasing the monsters off! (ROAR!!!!)

Doing the monster stomp!

ROAR   GRROWLL!

GOING AWAY

Going away, I'm going away, I'm going away from home.
I'm going away, I'm going away, I'm going away from home.
But before I leave, there are some things I'm gonna need:

Got my soap, and towel, and toothpaste, my sunscreen, and my shoes,
my name sewn in my underwear, so no one gets confused.
Leave my turtle for my brother, teach him how to feed my snakes,
make sure that my grandmother knows where to send the cupcakes.

I'm going away, I'm going away, I'm going away from home.
Going away, I'm going away, I'm going away from home.
But before I'm through, there are some things I've gotta do:

Take the TV from my grandpa's room and all his DVDs
'cause I may not come back so soon, a day or two at least.
Take my Aunt Sally's harmonica that I might learn to play,
and the blue t-shirt with the hole in the shoulder that I wear every day.

I'm going away, I'm going away, I'm going away from home.
I'm going away, I'm going away, I'm going away from home.
But before I leave, there are some things I'm gonna need.
Before I'm through, there are some things I've gotta do:

Got my soap, and towel, and toothpaste, my sunscreen, and my shoes,
my name sewn in my underwear, so no one gets confused.
Leave my turtle for my brother, teach him how to feed my snakes.
My address for my grandmother so that she can mail me cupcakes,
the t-shirt and the TV, the harmonica and DVDs
'cause I don't know what I might need; I might be gone a week.

Alarm clock, pet rock, my easy chair, sweat socks, headphones, stopwatch,
book about Sasquatch, spray paint, compass, a cushion for my rumpus,
a ladle, and a radio, and Oreos, and I know, my dad bought me a flashlight,
some ointment for a bug bite, a pen so maybe I'll write home.
All right . . .

Going away, I'm going away, I'm going away from home.
I'm going away, I'm going away, I'm going away from home.
But before I leave, there are some things I'm gonna need.
Before I'm through, there are some things I've gotta do.
I'm going away for forever and a day.
I'm going away from home.

CAMP LISA

Do Your Ears Hang Low?

B A A A A A A H

Put your hands up near
your head as though they
were great, big ears so you
can act out this silly song!

Do your ears hang low?
Do they wobble to and fro?
Can you tie them in a knot?
Can you tie them in a bow?
Can you throw them over your shoulder
like a Continental soldier?
Do your ears hang low?

hang low

wobble to

and fro

knot

bow

throw 'em over
your shoulder

hang low

Do your ears hang high?
Do they reach up to the sky?
Do they droop when they are wet?
Do they stiffen when they're dry?
Can you semaphore* your neighbor
with a minimum of labor?
Do your ears hang high?

*send messages with flags or poles

Do your ears hang out?
Can you waggle them about?
Can you flip them up and down
as you fly around the town?
Can you shut them up for sure
when you hear an awful bore?
Do your ears hang out?

Do your ears flip-flop?
Can you use them for a mop?
Are they stringy at the bottom?
Are they curly at the top?
Can you use them for a swatter?
Can you use them for a blotter?
Do your ears flip-flop?

EVERYBODY WAKE UP!

I was always a night owl, but at summer camp (and on school days), we had to wake up with the sun. YAWN!

Everybody wake up! Wake up!
Everybody wake up! Wake up!

Open your eyes! Jump out of bed!
Open your eyes! Jump out of bed!
If you're on the bottom bunk,
don't bump your head!

Everybody wake up! Wake up!
Everybody wake up! Wake up!

Find your shoes! Find your shoes!
Find your shoes! Find your other sock!
Don't hit the snooze on your alarm clock!

(RISE AND SHINE!)

Everybody wake up! Wake up!
Everybody wake up! Wake up!
Everybody wake up! Wake up!
Everybody wake up! Wake up!

Toothbrush, toothpaste, now wash your face.
Roll out, sound off.
It's time to get up, you gotta get up,
it's time to get up this morning!

THIS SONG HAS SOME MOVES THAT CAN MAKE SINGING ALONG AND EVEN WAKING UP MORE FUN.

{ CHORUS }

Use these motions for the chorus:

STOMP {left foot} → Everybody	CLAP → wake

STOMP {right foot} → up!	CLAP → wake

STOMP {left foot} → wake	CLAP → up!

{ VERSES }

Use these motions for the verses:

Open your eyes

Jump out of bed

Don't bump your head

Find your shoes

Find your sock

Don't hit the snooze on your alarm clock

Toothbrush, toothpaste

Wash your face

It's time to get up this morning!

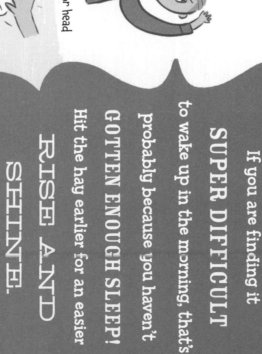

If you are finding it
SUPER DIFFICULT
to wake up in the morning, that's probably because you haven't
GOTTEN ENOUGH SLEEP!
Hit the hay earlier for an easier

RISE AND SHINE.

Hello, Today

Growing up, I loved taking dance lessons, where I learned about stretching and moving and breathing. When I take yoga classes, I practice these same things. My friends Michelle and Dan and I decided it would be really exciting (and relaxing and energizing) to write a song that weaves together some yoga-inspired moves.

Stand up, wave to the sun,
breathe in deep 'cause the day's begun.
Head high, hands open wide,
look to the sky and say,

Breathe out, breathe in,
the day is new, we'll start again.
Breathe in, breathe out,
head is up, your shoulders down.

"Hey, good morning. Hello, today."
Smile at the sunshine and say,
"Hello, today."

Breathe out, let your hands down,
bow to the ground below.
Then grow, grow up like a tree,
breezy and green and light.

Back to the start,
hands at your heart,
feet stand apart and strong.
Say thanks to yourself,
thanks to your friends,
and thanks to your morning song.

"Hey, good morning. Hello, today."
Smile at the sunshine and say,
"Hello, today."

"Hey, good morning. Hello, today."
Smile at the sunshine and say,
"Hello, today."

STAND UP

Stand tall,
shoulders relaxed,
big toes touching

WAVE TO THE SUN

Arms up high,
look at the sky,
and breathe in deeply

HANDS DOWN

Arms at your
sides, head level,
breathe out

BOW

Keep legs straight,
bow as low
as you can

This set of movements is called the

SUN SALUTATION.

It started a very long time ago in India as a way to begin the day and appreciate **THE POWER AND ENERGY OF THE SUN.**

Breathing deeply is just as important as the movements, so **DON'T FORGET TO BREATHE!**

ROLL UP

Roll up slowly—
your head
comes up last

TREE

Plant your feet firmly,
like roots, and stand up
very straight

HEART

Put your palms
together at your heart,
fingers pointing up

Peanut Butter AND Jelly

BON APPÉTIT

Peanut, peanut butter, and jelly.
Peanut, peanut butter, and jelly.

First you take the peanuts and you pick 'em,
you pick 'em, you pick 'em, pick 'em, pick 'em,
and you smash 'em, you smash 'em,
you smash 'em, smash 'em, smash 'em,
and you spread 'em, you spread 'em,
you spread 'em, spread 'em, spread 'em.

Peanut, peanut butter, and jelly.
Peanut, peanut butter, and jelly.

There are lots of fun movements that go with this delicious song. You can reach up high or way down low to pick the peanuts and the grapes, and then use your fist to smash them in one hand, and spread them on that same hand as though it were a piece of bread. Or maybe you'd rather stomp on them with your feet! Be sure to do something snazzy with your hands every time you sing the word "jelly" in the chorus. You can even say "jelly" in a funny, growly voice.

Then you take the grapes and you pick 'em,
you pick 'em, you pick 'em, pick 'em, pick 'em,
and you smash 'em, you smash 'em,
you smash 'em, smash 'em, smash 'em,
and you spread 'em, you spread 'em,
you spread 'em, spread 'em, spread 'em.

Peanut, peanut butter, and jelly.
Peanut, peanut butter, and jelly.

Then you take the sandwich and you bite it,
you bite it, you bite it, bite it, bite it,
and you chew it, you chew it,
you chew it, chew it, chew it,
and you swallow it, you swallow it,
you swallow it, swallow it, swallow it.

Mmm, Mmm, Mmm, Mmm.
Mmm, Mmm, Mmm, Mmm.

CHOMP

"

Your mouth is still full of
GOOEY PEANUT BUTTER,
so instead of singing the words
to the chorus this time,
HUM THE TUNE WITH YOUR
LIPS SEALED.

Head, Shoulders, Knees, and Toes

T his is a song you can sing, without any instruments, anywhere you can move around. It's fun to speed it up as you go, and I can almost guarantee that you'll end up laughing like crazy as you try to remember which words to sing and which words to leave out!

HERE'S HOW IT WORKS:

Each time you sing "head," touch your head with your hands. When you sing "shoulders," touch your shoulders. And so on! With each verse, you start NOT saying one part at a time, and say "hmmm" instead. Little by little, all of the names of the parts disappear, but you still go through the motions, humming through the blanks.

Head, shoulders, knees, and toes,
knees and toes.
Head, shoulders, knees, and toes,
knees and toes.
and eyes, and ears, and mouth, and nose.
Head, shoulders, knees, and toes,
knees and toes!

Hmmm, shoulders, knees, and toes,
knees and toes.
Hmmm, shoulders, knees, and toes,
knees and toes,
and eyes, and ears, and mouth, and nose.
Hmmm, shoulders, knees, and toes,
knees and toes!

Hmmm, hmm-hmm, knees, and toes,
knees and toes.
Hmmm, hmm-hmm, knees, and toes,
knees and toes,
and eyes, and ears, and mouth, and nose.
Hmmm, hmm-hmm, knees, and toes,
knees and toes!

Hmmm, hmmm, hmmm, hmmm, hmmm,
hmmm, hmmm.
Hmmm, hmmm-hmmm, hmmm, hmmm,
hmm, hmmm,
and eyes, and ears, and mouth, and nose.
Hmmm, hmmm-hmmm, hmmm, hmmm,
hmm, hmmm!

Hmmm, hmmm, hmmm, hmmm, hmmm,
hmmm, hmmm.
Hmmm, hmmm-hmmm, hmmm, hmmm,
hmmm, hmmm,
hmmm, hmmm, mouth, and nose.
Hmmm, hmmm-hmmm, hmmm, hmmm,
hmm, hmmm!

hmmm, hmmm, hmmm, toes,
hmm toes.
Hmmm, hmmm-hmmm, hmmm, toes,
hmm toes,
and eyes, and ears, and mouth, and nose.
Hmmm, hmmm-hmmm, hmmm, toes,
hmm, toes!

Hmmm, hmmm-hmmm, hmmm, hmmm,
hmm, hmmm.
Hmmm, hmmm-hmmm, hmmm, hmmm,
hmm, hmmm,
and eyes, and ears, and mouth, and nose.
Hmmm, hmmm-hmmm, hmmm, hmmm,
hmm, hmmm!

Hmmm, hmmm-hmmm, hmmm, hmmm,
hmm, hmmm.
Hmmm, hmmm-hmmm, hmmm, hmmm,
hmm, hmmm,
hmm, ears, and mouth, and nose.
Hmmm, hmmm-hmmm, hmmm, hmmm,
hmm, hmmm!

CREDITS

TURN IT DOWN! +
(The Air Band Song)
Written by Lisa Loeb, Dan Petty,
and Michelle Lewis
Furious Rose Music (BMI), Bambalam
Music (BMI), Bea the Dog Music (ASCAP)
Vocals, rhythm guitar: Lisa Loeb
Percussion, jazz flute, keyboard:
Dan Petty
Bass: Curt Schneider
Drums: Blair Sinta
Background vocals: Michelle Lewis

FATHER ABRAHAM +
Vocals: Lisa Loeb and the
Morning Campers
Accoustic Guitar: Lisa Loeb
Harmonies: Michelle Lewis
Tambourine: Dan Petty

MISS MARY MACK +
Vocals: Lisa Loeb and Michelle Lewis

MONSTER STOMP +
Written by Lisa Loeb, Dan Petty,
and Michelle Lewis
Furious Rose Music (BMI), Bambalam
Music (BMI), Bea the Dog Music (ASCAP)
Vocals: Lisa Loeb and the Afternoon Campers
Guitars, drums, bass, and organ:
Dan Petty

CONTACT:
Lisa Loeb,
11054 Ventura Blvd. #381,
Studio City, CA 91604
Visit Lisa at
www.lisaloeb.com
and follow her on
Twitter @LisaLoeb

GOING AWAY *
Written by Lisa Loeb, Dan Petty,
and Michelle Lewis
Furious Rose Music (BMI), Bambalam
Music (BMI), Bea the Dog Music (ASCAP)
Vocals: Lisa Loeb
Vocals, acoustic guitar: Dan Petty
Bass: Leland Sklar
Drums: Jay Bellerose
Piano: Doug Petty
Harmonies, kazoo: Michelle Lewis

DO YOUR EARS HANG LOW? +
Vocals, acoustic guitar: Lisa Loeb

EVERYBODY WAKE UP! +
Written by Lisa Loeb, Dan Petty,
and Michelle Lewis
Furious Rose Music (BMI), Bambalam
Music (BMI), Bea the Dog Music (ASCAP)
Vocals, claps, and stomps: Lisa Loeb and
Michelle Lewis
Everything else and whatnots: Dan Petty

HELLO, TODAY +
Written by Lisa Loeb, Dan Petty,
and Michelle Lewis
Furious Rose Music (BMI), Bambalam
Music (BMI), Bea the Dog Music (ASCAP)
Vocals, acoustic guitar: Lisa Loeb
Acoustic guitar: Dan Petty

PEANUT BUTTER AND JELLY +
Vocals: Lisa Loeb and the Morning
Campers

HEAD, SHOULDERS,
KNEES, & TOES +
Vocals: Lisa Loeb
Keyboard, percussion, and sound effects:
Dan Petty

Morning Campers:
Hayden Begley, Henry Eisenstein,
Zoe Eisenstein, Arden Kelly, Georgica
Pettus, Harry Pettus, Isabel Petty,
Trystin Saure

Afternoon Campers:
Henry Eisenstein, Zoe Eisenstein,
Georgica Pettus, Harry Pettus,
Isabel Petty, Olive Petty

Produced by Lisa Loeb, Dan Petty,
and Michelle Lewis
Recorded and Engineered by Dan Petty
at The Path, Valley Village, CA

+ Mixed by Dan Petty
* Mixed by Bob Clearmountain, Mix This!
Mix This! Assistant: Brandon Duncan

Mastered by Hans DeKline

Special thanks to Meredith Mundy, Kim
Marini, Merideth Harte, Jennifer Browning,
Caitlin Friedman, Gayatri Mullapudi, Katie
Connors, and everyone at Sterling.

Management: Janet Billig Rich,
Manage This!
Legal Representation: Adam Ritholz,
Ritholz, Levy, Sanders, Chidikel
& Fields LLP
Business Management: Carrie Malcolm with
Yana Romano, CRM Management LLC

For more information on the Camp Lisa
Foundation, go to www.camplisa.com

The Camp Lisa Foundation proudly
supports Summer Camp Opportunities
Provide an Edge, Inc. (SCOPE), a nonprofit
organization providing children in need the
edge to succeed in life through the summer
camp experience. www.scope-ny.org